Why Am I Different?

Norma Simon

Pictures by Dora Leder

Albert Whitman & Company, Morton Grove, Illinois

*For my friends in the Wellfleet Elementary School and
Becky and Emily Bleifield, too. Thank you for all your help.*
N. S.

Library of Congress Cataloging-in-Publication Data

Simon, Norma.
    Why am I different?
    (Concept books)
    Summary: Portrays everyday situations in which
children see themselves as "different" in family life,
preferences, and aptitudes, and yet, feel that being
different is all right.
    1. Individuality—Juvenile literature.
[1.Individuality] I. Leder, Dora. II. Title.
BF697.S548 155.2 76-41172
ISBN 0-8075-9074-6 (lib. bdg.)
ISBN 0-8075-9076-2 (pbk.)

CORINNE LIGHT

A Note About Growing

The gradual development of a realistic self-image is a critical area of child growth. It is knowing who you are and how you feel about the very special person you happen to be.

In gaining this identity of self, comparison plays a part. Children measure themselves against others, comparing height, hair color, place in the family, preferences, and abilities—to name a few familiar yardsticks. Being like someone else may become extremely desirable. Good friends want to look alike, dress alike, share fun and experiences.

Comparison, recognition, and analysis lead girls and boys to be aware of differences which involve themselves and others. The child weighs perceived positive and negative values and uses this new awareness as growth continues.

This book shows everyday ways in which children see themselves as different. Discussion between adults and children is almost certain to bring up other examples of differences. Girls and boys frequently seek reasons for what they observe, asking the intelligent and inevitable "Why?" Sometimes reasons can be given. Sometimes differences exist for which there are no apparent reasons.

Adult reassurance helps the girl or boy who feels different and who is thought by the group to be unlike the others in some way. This reassurance plays a significant role in interpreting this sensitive area. The way is paved for acceptance and respect for each individual and for healthy self-respect.

Differences make our world more interesting, colorful, and richer than it would be if everyone were alike. This book helps children feel pride in the specialness of "Being me!"

I'm different!
I'm getting a big front tooth.
What's different about you?

We're all different sizes
at school.
Look how big Greg is.
Look how small Libby is.
And I'm right in-between.

8

But at home, I'm the biggest kid.

My mother and my brothers
all have blond hair.
My father and my sister have
brown hair.
Why am I different?
My hair is red.

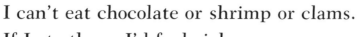

I can't eat chocolate or shrimp or clams.
If I ate them, I'd feel sick.
I wonder if they taste as good as people say.
I don't like being different about eating.

People can do different things.
You draw better pictures than I do.
I can write better than you.
That's how I'm different.
Charlie's fastest with puzzles.
Cindy can whistle. And remember
how good Kearsten is at cutting
out snowflakes?

13

Everyone wanted to dress up like a ghost
for the Halloween parade.
I like to be different.
My father helped me—I was a robot.
I was different, all right.

My sister wants different things for
her birthday than I want for mine.
She wants a baseball and a book about horses.
I want roller skates and a bracelet.

Everybody I know lives in a house
with an elevator.
My house is different—it has stairs.
But I like to ride with my friends
in their elevators.

Do you know anybody else without a TV?
My mother and father don't want one.
Why do they have to be different?
I see some good shows at my friend's house.

18

My family is different.
We don't have a car.
Mom and I take the bus.
You can go lots of places that way.

My grandma doesn't just visit us.
She lives in our house.
It's nice having a grandma around.
I'm glad I'm different.

It's different for me when I want to see
my grandma.
I have to fly in a big plane.
Grandma and Grandpa live in Puerto Rico.
Everybody talks Spanish. I do, too.

It's different when you move a lot.
We go from house to house and from town to town.
That way I know different kids all the time.
And I go to different schools.
Sometimes I feel kind of different myself.

When my mother puts some matzos
in my lunchbox, the other kids say,
"What's that? What's that?"
They know, but they like to show
I'm different.

I told my mother, "Please make
macaroni and cheese or brownies
for the school supper."
She made something different.
Everybody loved it.

We're all different in lots of ways.
Here's another way.
Our mothers and fathers do different
kinds of work.

My baby sister is adopted.
So am I.
Do you think that makes us different?
Maybe, but we love each other.

I'm the only kid in my family.
That makes me different.
Sometimes it's OK,
and sometimes it isn't.

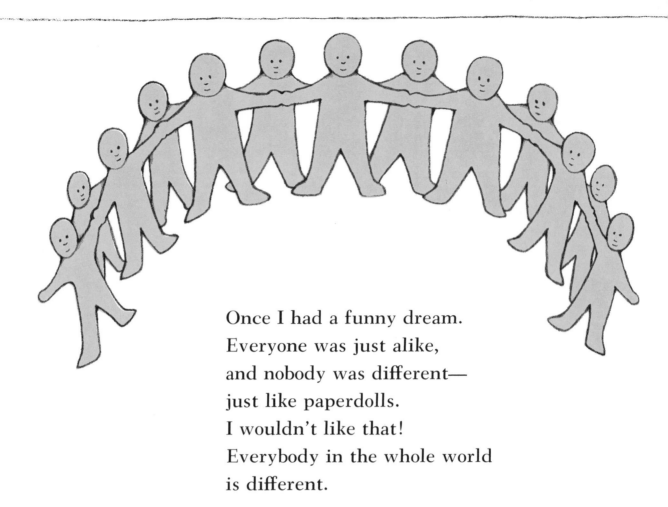

Once I had a funny dream.
Everyone was just alike,
and nobody was different—
just like paperdolls.
I wouldn't like that!
Everybody in the whole world
is different.

Nobody's exactly like me.

You know something? We're different, but alike, too.
We eat and play and wear clothes and live in houses.
But I'm not you, and you're not me.
I think different things, I feel different things.
I know different things, and I do different things.
I look different.

I *am* different. And so are you. That's good!

Using This Book

What does it mean to be different? How do we feel about it? The situations shown in this book have been carefully chosen to help explore these questions. The examples reflect familiar, widely shared experiences and may help girls and boys talk about feelings concerned with knowing one's self and one's relation to others.

There is a progression of underlying concepts, leading to the positive view of differences as factors which make lives rich and interesting. Differences related to growth (pages 7 to 9) are given first because physical growth concerns all children. Traits which are hereditary, such as hair color (page 10), follow, and specific physical conditions, such as allergies and food sensitivities, are touched upon (page 11).

Other factors which make us dissimilar grow out of different kinds of abilities (pages 12–13) and individual preferences (pages 14 and 15). We are shaped by home and neighborhood experiences (page 16–17) and family standards and circumstances (pages 18 and 19). Families are not alike in composition (pages 20 and 21), while mobility or lack of it has consequences (pages 22–23).

Children grow up with different ethnic, religious, and cultural backgrounds which enhance their lives (pages 24 and 25). The occupations of parents are of significance, too (pages 26–27). And there are sometimes special circumstances, such as being adopted or an only child (pages 28 and 29) which make a girl or boy feel set apart.

Would the world be a better place if there were no differences? Children readily agree it would not. And the strength of our culture, as we as a people believe, is in our diversity and the wealth of our individual contributions. Self-respect and respect for others—these are the goals we hope our children will achieve.

CORINNE LIGHT